My Abilities

Andrea Brown
Illustrated by Dwight Nacaytuna

Copyright © 2016 by Andrea Brown. 746170

ISBN: Softcover   978-1-5245-4348-8
        EBook   978-1-5245-4347-1

All rights reserved. No part of this book may
be reproduced or transmitted in any form or by
any means, electronic or mechanical, including
photocopying, recording, or by any information storage
and retrieval system, without permission in writing from
the copyright owner.

This is a work of fiction. Names, characters,
places and incidents either are the product of the
author's imagination or are used fictitiously, and any
resemblance to any actual persons, living or dead,
events, or locales is entirely coincidental.

Print information available on the last page

Rev. date: 09/14/2016

To order additional copies of this book, contact:
Xlibris
1-888-795-4274
www.Xlibris.com
Orders@Xlibris.com

My Abilities

Andrea Brown
Illustrated by Dwight Nacaytuna

Kymmaina was born without hearing. Kymmaina's ability is using sign language. She is light brown in complexion. Blonde hair, blue eyes.

Keo was born with limited vision. Keo uses a walking cane to help him get around. Keo also uses a Braille type writer for his home work. Keo is Chinese.

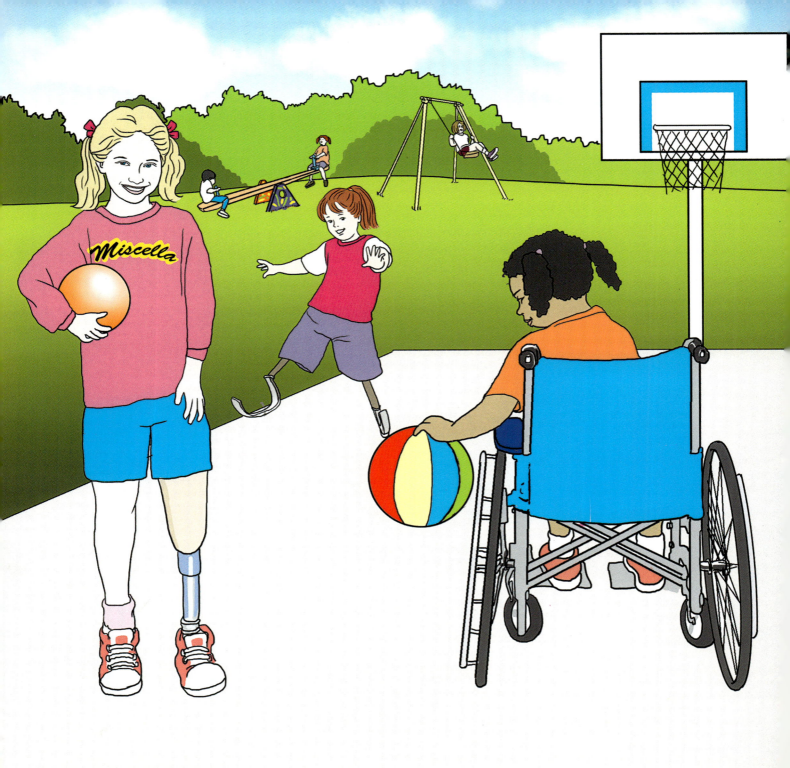

Miscella loses one leg to cancer at 8 years old. Miscella have a special leg to help her walk and run. Miscella is Caucasian.

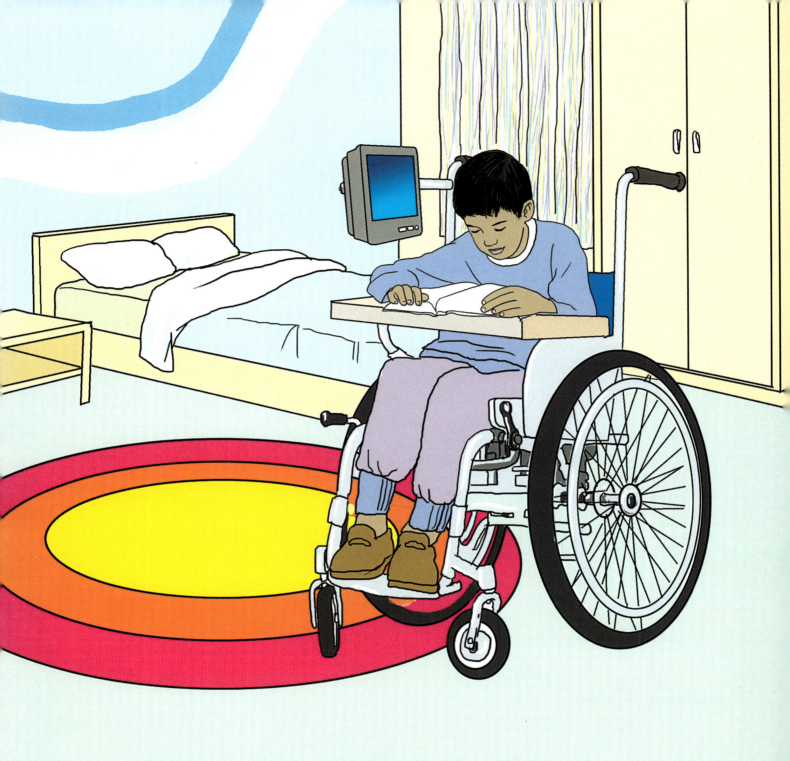

My name is Tamilo. I cannot speak.
Only with my voice machine. I
was born with cerebral palsy. I
am Indian.

Andy was born with a brain tumor. Andy have some vision and walking mobility and use a seeing eye dog to get to work. Andy is Caucasian.

Shaman was born with down syndrome. Shaman works in a grocery stock store. Shaman is inter racial.

Hidella was born with one hand. Hidella uses a special hand to help her do more things like cleaning and lifting. Hidella is African.

Christian was born with a learning disability. Christian attends a special needs class to help him learn to write and read better. Christian is inter racial.

Marie was born with diabetes. She has some walking difficulties. Marie uses a walker to help her exercise. Marie is Caucasian.

Jailyn was born with muscular dystrophy. Jailyn is unable to walk. Jailyn is a baker. She is African American.

Edwards Brothers Malloy
Thorofare, NJ USA
December 29, 2016